For Lena, I love you —A.W.P.

Especially for my studio dog, Sadie —D.W.

Farrar Straus Giroux Books for Young Readers
An imprint of Macmillan Publishing Group, LLC
175 Fifth Avenue, New York, NY 10010

Text copyright © 2017 by Ann Whitford Paul
Pictures copyright © 2017 by David Walker
All rights reserved
Color separations by Bright Arts (H.K.) Ltd.
Printed in the United States of America by
Worzalla, Stevens Point, Wisconsin
Designed by Roberta Pressel
First edition, 2017
3 5 7 9 10 8 6 4 2

mackids.com

Library of Congress Cataloging-in-Publication Data

Names: Paul, Ann Whitford, author. | Walker, David, 1965- illustrator.
Title: If animals said I love you / Ann Whitford Paul ; pictures by David Walker.
Description: First edition. | New York : Farrar Straus Giroux, 2017. | A
Companion to: If Animals Kissed Good Night. | Summary: Imagines how
animals would say I love you.
Identifiers: LCCN 2016057827| ISBN 9780374306021 (hardcover) | ISBN
9780374306038 (board book)
Subjects: | CYAC: Animals—Habits and behavior—Fiction. | Families—Fiction.
| Love—Fiction. | Stories in rhyme.
Classification: LCC PZ8.3.P273645 Ifg 2017 | DDC [E]—dc23
LC record available at https://lccn.loc.gov/2016057827

Our books may be purchased in bulk for promotional, educational, or business use.
Please contact your local bookseller or the Macmillan Corporate and Premium Sales Department
at (800) 221-7945 ext. 5442 or by e-mail at MacmillanSpecialMarkets@macmillan.com.

If Animals Said I Love You

Ann Whitford Paul

Pictures by David Walker

Farrar Straus Giroux

New York

If animals said "I love you" like we do,
Gorilla would pound a loud chest, **slap-slap**.
"I love you, my young one."

Whappity-whap.

Whale would sing it and, from his spout,
shoot some heart-shaped bubbles out.

Boa would hiss, "Hatchlings, come please.
Time for a loving, squish-hugging squeeze."

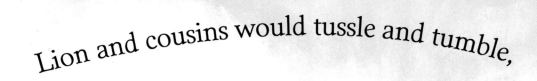

Lion and cousins would tussle and tumble,

romp and roll in a joyful love jumble.

If animals said "I love you" like we do,
Gorilla would say it and offer a treat.
"Bamboo, little infant! **Yum! Yum!** Eat!"

Secretary Bird would type with claw feet

LOVE YOU

warm, tender words with a **click-clack** beat.

Cheetah would murmur love's soft purr
and **lick, lick, lick** her sister's fur.

Scampering Spider, spinning his web,

would write "I adore you" in silky white thread.

If animals said "I love you" like we do,
Gorilla would say it and **pat-pat** her lap.
"Let me hold you close in my hairy arm wrap."

Ostrich would strut, his friends by his side,

booming his love with his feathers spread wide.

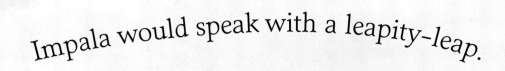

Impala would speak with a leapity-leap.

"I love you, my grandchild, a **heapity-heap**."

Alligator would add a big tail swish
and shower his brother—*splashity-splish*.

If animals said "I love *you*" like we do,
Gorilla and infant would **smoocheroo**,
then rumble with happiness loud and deep.

Sure of their love,
they'd snuggle and sleep.